LAND OF THE LOST TEDDIES

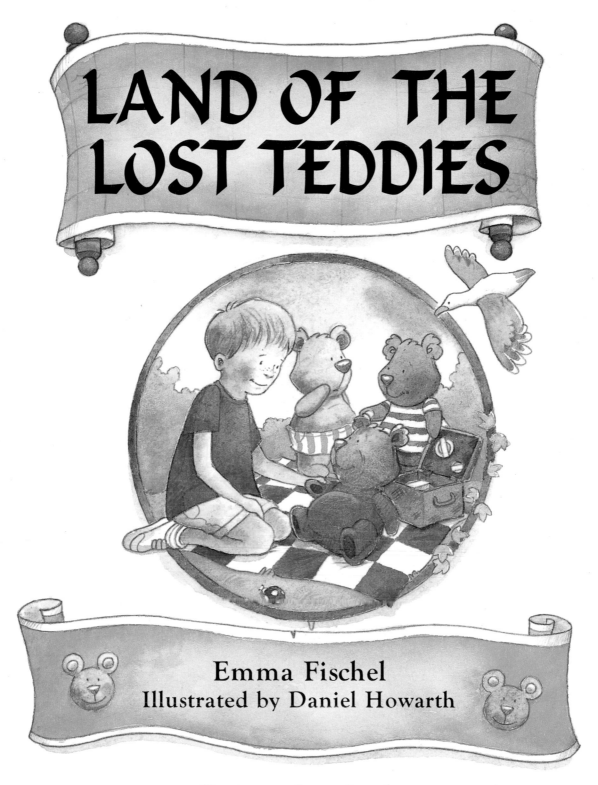

Emma Fischel
Illustrated by Daniel Howarth

Designer: Lucy Smith
Editor: Michelle Bates
Series Editor: Gaby Waters

Contents

Getting Ready

Wilfie and his teddy, Eddie, are getting ready for an exciting day out at Fun World. But little do they know just HOW exciting it will be. So turn the page and join them in a great adventure.

Where's Teddy?

Wilfie and his teddy, Eddie, did one exciting thing after another...

and another...

and another.

They even went looking
for sharks in the bay.

Then Wilfie noticed something was wrong.
"AAAAARGH!" he screamed. "Teddy's gone!"
Sure enough, Eddie had vanished, but
he'd left his shoe and his
sunglasses behind.

Can you spot them?

5

The Search Begins

Poor Wilfie! Nothing cheered him up – not even a visit to the toyshop.

"I don't want this teddy!" he said, sadly. "I want MY teddy."

"You could try looking in the Land of the Lost Teddies," said the friendly toyshop owner. "Most teddies go there when children lose them. It's full of the things teddies like best." He opened the green door behind him. "And you're in luck! There's a train going there right now."

"Now let's see," said the toyshop owner, scratching his head. "Which train is it? I know it has a shape on the front, but it's not a star. And it doesn't have a green funnel. Well, anyway, the engine is red."

Which train is off to the Land of the Lost Teddies?

On the Way

The conductor blew her whistle, and soon they were off. Slowly they chugged through a magical world, past Spook Castle and Jelly Town.

"How many more stops before we get there?" cried Wilfie as they approached the Dinosaur Park.

"It's just the other side of the tunnel," said the conductor. "Not far to go now."

How many more stops do they have to make?

Which Way Now?

At last the train stopped at the Land of the Lost Teddies. Wilfie gasped. How was he ever going to find his teddy here? There were teddies EVERYWHERE.

And there were certainly plenty of things for a teddy to do. Wilfie didn't know where to begin to look for Eddie. Then he spotted something that gave him a clue to where Eddie had gone.

What has Wilfie seen? (It's one of a pair, and Wilfie has the other one!)

11

Picnic Path

Wilfie hurried along the path until he reached a big iron gate. He read the notice and beamed. His teddy loved picnics. Maybe he'd find Eddie there.

Wilfie pushed open the gate. What a lot of winding paths! By the time he found a way through them, the picnic would probably be over!

Can you help Wilfie get to the picnic?

PICNIC TODAY IN MIDDLE OF MAZE start at the red flag

START

Teddy Bears' Picnic

It was just the sort of picnic Eddie liked.
There was lots of food, lots of fun and,
of course, lots of teddies.

Wilfie could see big teddies, small teddies,
old teddies... but not HIS teddy.

He took out his photo of Eddie.
Perhaps someone had seen him.

"We remember him," a yellow teddy said. "Who wouldn't? He had four slices of pizza, two ice creams, a banana milkshake, three strawberry tartlets AND the last slice of chocolate cake."

"Yes, and I wanted that too," sniffed a purple teddy.

FIND THE ODD ONE OUT

"We'll tell you where he went but please help us with our picnic puzzle first. We can't agree on the answer."

Which clown is the odd one out?

Bear Trouble

"He went off to the lake," said the purple teddy. "There's a short cut through the maze to it."

"But watch out. It's easy to get lost, and if you do, you'll be heading for Bear Mountain," the other teddy added with a shiver. "And we're talking big bears. VERY big bears."

"Oh dear," said Wilfie, as he went around in circles. "I think I must be lost."

It began to rain. It grew colder... and colder.

It began to snow. It grew steeper... and steeper.

OOPS! Wilfie bumped into something.
Something very large.
Something very furry.
Something like a VERY BIG BEAR.
Help! thought Wilfie. What's it going
to do?

ROAR?

OR EAT ME?

The Bear Cave

The bear wasn't scary at all.

"OUCH!" he sniffed, holding out his paw.

Gently Wilfie pulled a huge, thorn out of its paw.

"Oh thank you," the bear said, smiling. "Now you must come to tea. Hop on my back."

What a ride! They galloped mile after mile through the softly falling snow. Wilfie clung on tightly to the bear's warm fur.

Then the bear stopped at the mouth of a big dark cave. "Welcome to my home," he said.

Wilfie soon told the bear all about his teddy. "I've met him," said the bear. "He was going to catch a boat to Mermaid Island. I took him to the lake. He gave me something when he left."

Can you see what Eddie gave the bear?

By the Lake

After a big plate of buns and honey the bear took Wilfie down the mountain to the lake.

They waved goodbye to each other at the water's edge.

There were boats everywhere, bobbing gently in the waves.

"There are three boats free, but only one of them goes to Mermaid Island," said the boatkeeper, pointing at the pictures on his big board.

Which boat can Wilfie take to Mermaid Island?

Mermaid Island

Wilfie set off as fast as he
could. At last, arms aching,
he reached Mermaid Island.
He searched for Eddie

high...

... and low.

Found him! he thought.

But he was wrong.
It was a merteddy!

"I'm looking for my teddy. Have you seen him?"
Wilfie asked, showing the merteddy Eddie's photo.
"I think he went that way." The little creature
pointed to the shore. "One of those pink snapping
crabs just took a chunk out of his shorts."

**Can you find a safe way to the shore
without stepping on any rocks with crabs?**

23

Another Clue

Wilfie searched left and right as he trudged up the road.
It would be dark soon. Would he EVER find Eddie?
Then he saw a little pair of yellow shorts
sticking out of a litter bin. They
were Eddie's.

SLEEPY SAM'S
PJ STALL

SWEETS

BURGERS

HOSPITAL
NURSERY
PLAYGROUND

ICES ICES

"Eddie's shorts had a hole in them," explained the teddy at the clothes stall. "He was very sleepy, so he was going to the nursery for a rest. He wanted a new sleepsuit to wear. He was most particular. He wanted stripes, but not yellow. He loved blue, but not with red, and he didn't want anything green."

"I know what he chose," smiled Wilfie.

Can you find an outfit like the one Eddie chose?

25

Bedtime Story

Wilfie ran to the nursery as fast as he could. He knocked very loudly, but there was no answer. With a trembling hand, he pushed open the little wooden door. Would he find Eddie at last?

Wilfie could see sleepy teds tucked up in bed. He could see soapy teds splashing in bubbles. He could see story-time teds listening to a tale. And best of all, Wilfie could see HIS ted!

Can you see Eddie? Do you recognize the person reading the story?

Teddy's Story

Wilfie hugged Eddie as tight as he could.
"What happened to you?" he asked. "How
did you get here?"
Eddie made himself comfy on Wilfie's
knee, and then he began to tell his story...

A huge seagull snatched
me up.

He dropped me as soon as he
realized I wasn't a nice juicy fish.

I landed on a porpoise. He took
me to shore.

I found a train
station, but no one
was around.

There was a box of blankets.
I nodded off in it.

I woke up on a train. It was going to
the Land of the Lost Teddies.

Then Eddie gave a big yawn.

"Now that you've found each other,
it's time to go home," the toyshop owner
said to Wilfie. "And I have a present for
each of you." He scratched his head.
"Now where did I put them?"

Can you spot the presents?

Homeward Bound

Wilfie and Eddie waved goodbye and boarded the train. Soon they were leaving the Land of the Lost Teddies far behind them.

Inside the presents, Wilfie found lots of things to remind him of their day, and best of all, he had Eddie back to share them with.

Answers

Pages 4-5
Eddie's shoe and sunglasses are circled below.

Pages 6-7
This is the train that is off to the Land of the Lost Teddies.

Pages 8-9
There are four stops ahead of them, including the one for the Dinosaur Park. You will find them circled below.

Pages 10-11
Wilfie has spotted Eddie's shoe. Here it is.

Pages 12-13
The way through to the picnic is shown here.

Pages 14-15
The clown circled below is the odd one out.

Pages 18-19
Eddie gave the bear his badge. Here it is.

Pages 20-21
Wilfie should take the boat circled below to get to Mermaid Island.

Pages 22-23
The safe way to the shore is marked here.

Pages 24-25
Eddie chose this outfit.

Pages 26-27
Eddie is here. The person reading the story is the toyshop owner!

Pages 28-29
The presents are circled below.

First published in 1997 by Usborne Publishing Ltd, Usborne House, 83-85 Saffron Hill, London EC1N 8RT, England.
Copyright © 1997 Usborne Publishing Ltd.
The name Usborne and the device ⊕ are Trade Marks of Usborne Publishing Ltd.
All rights reserved.